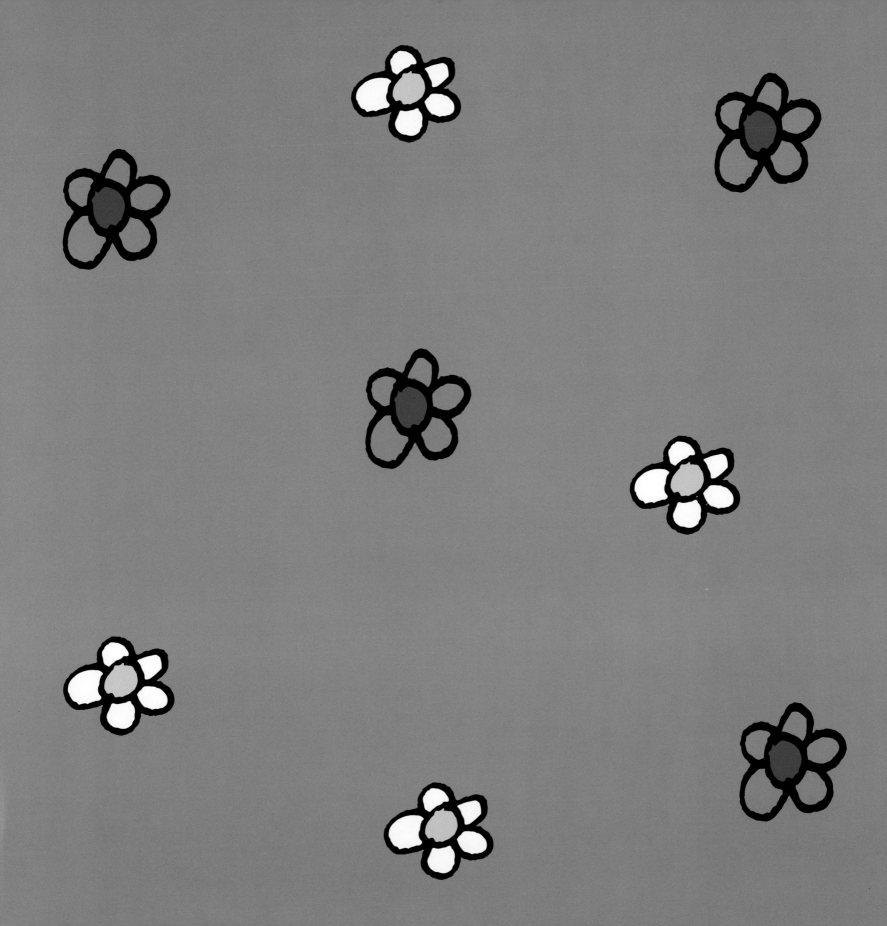

sheep has lost her noise!

does sheep say ribbet, ribbet?

that's my noise

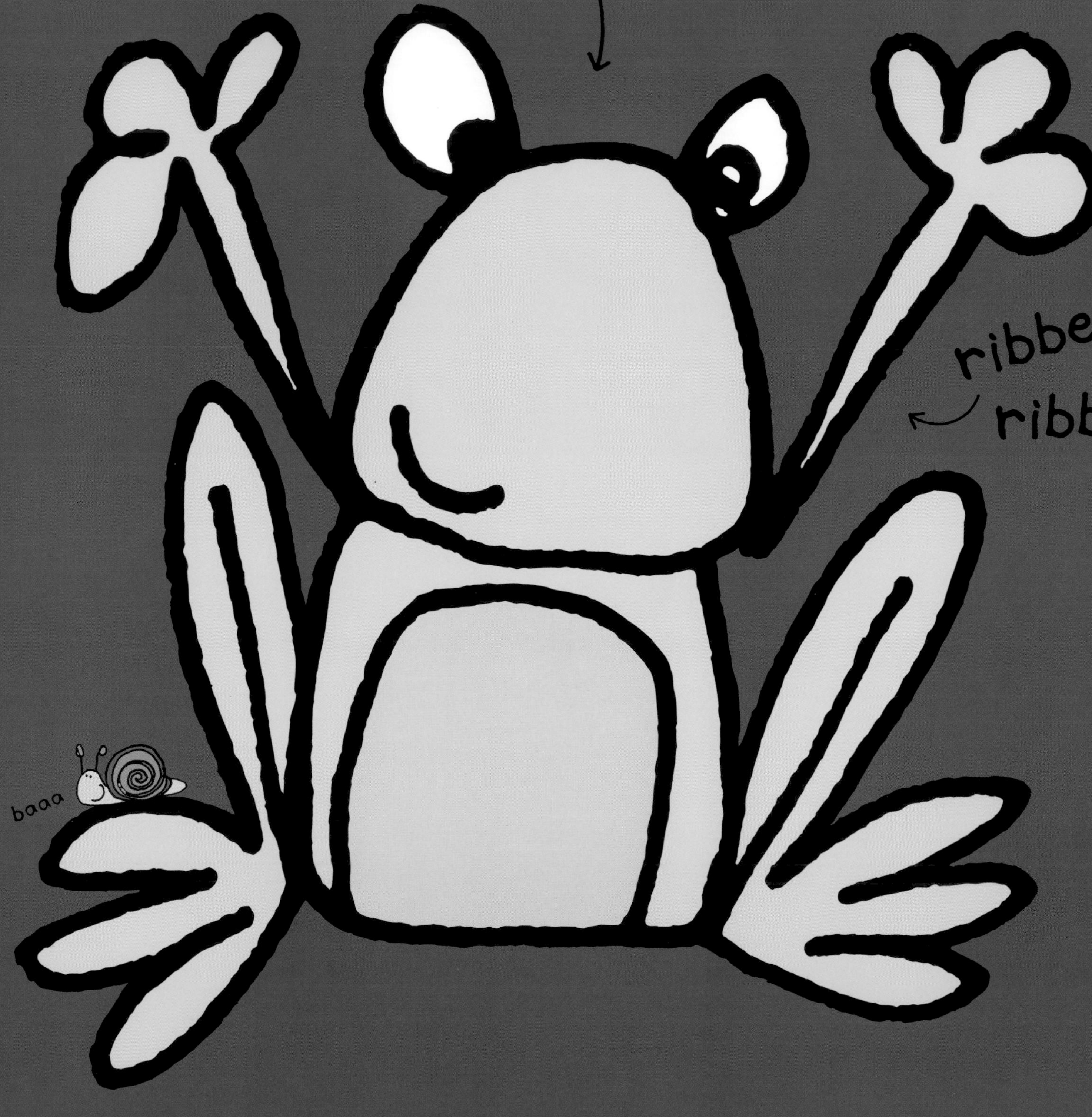

ribbet
ribbet

no, frog says
ribbet, ribbet!

does sheep say
oink, oink?

no, pig says
oink, oink!

does sheep say
woof, woof?

no, shaggy dog says
woof, woof!

does sheep say
moooooooooo?

no, COW says

mooooooooo!

does sheep say

miaow, miaow?

no, tabby cat says
miaow, miaow!

does sheep say
neigh, neigh?

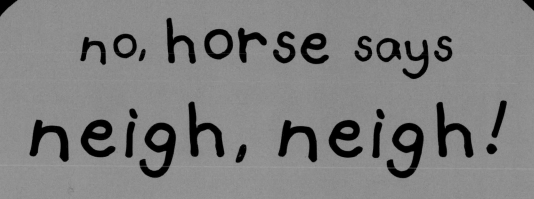

no, horse says
neigh, neigh!

what does sheep say?

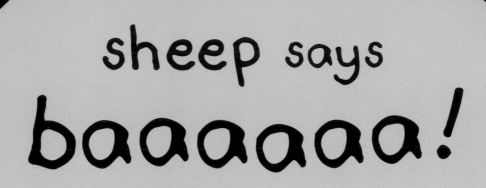

sheep says

baaaaaa!

what noise do
you make?

can you see who helped find sheep's baa?

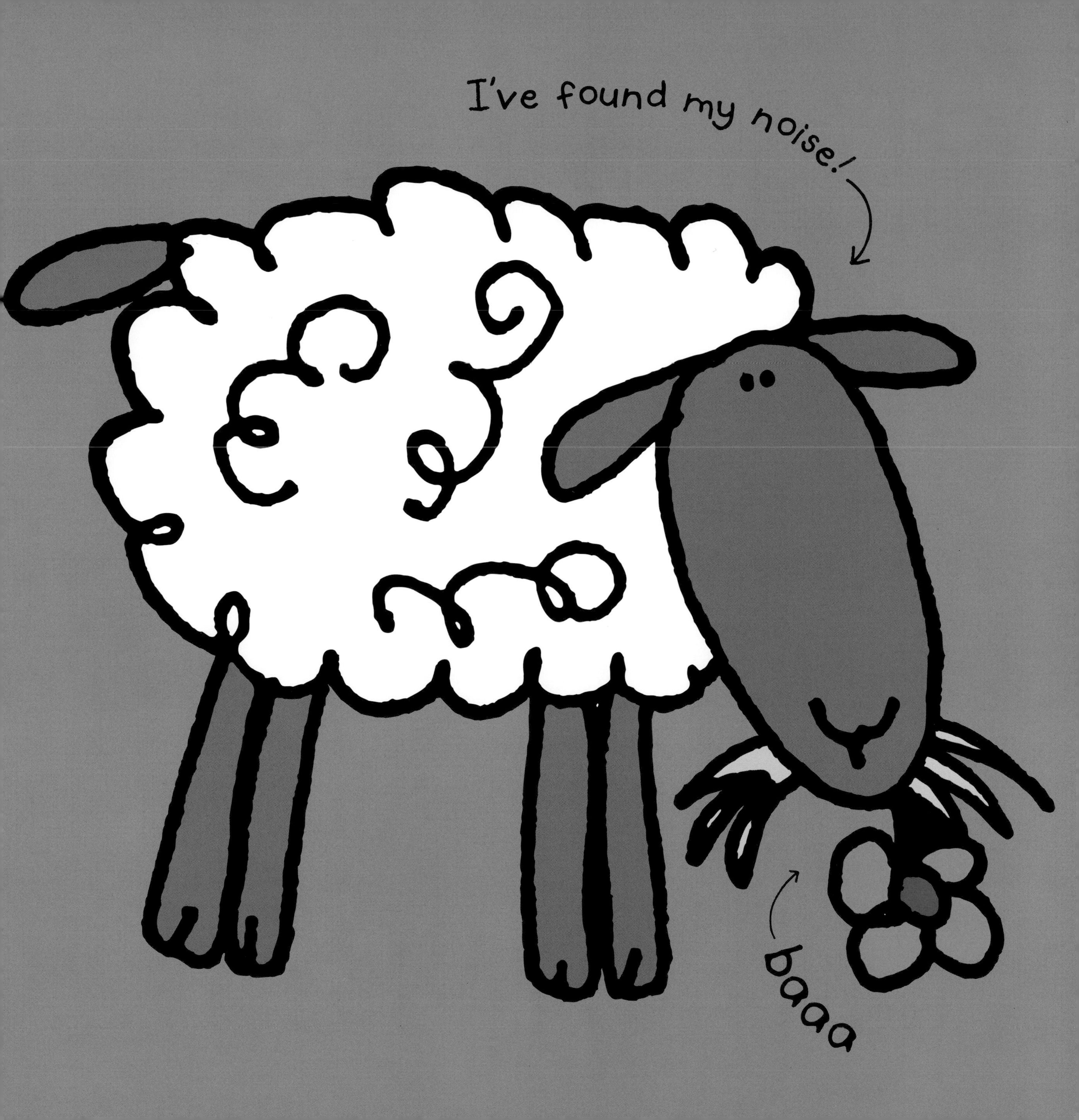
I've found my noise!
baaa

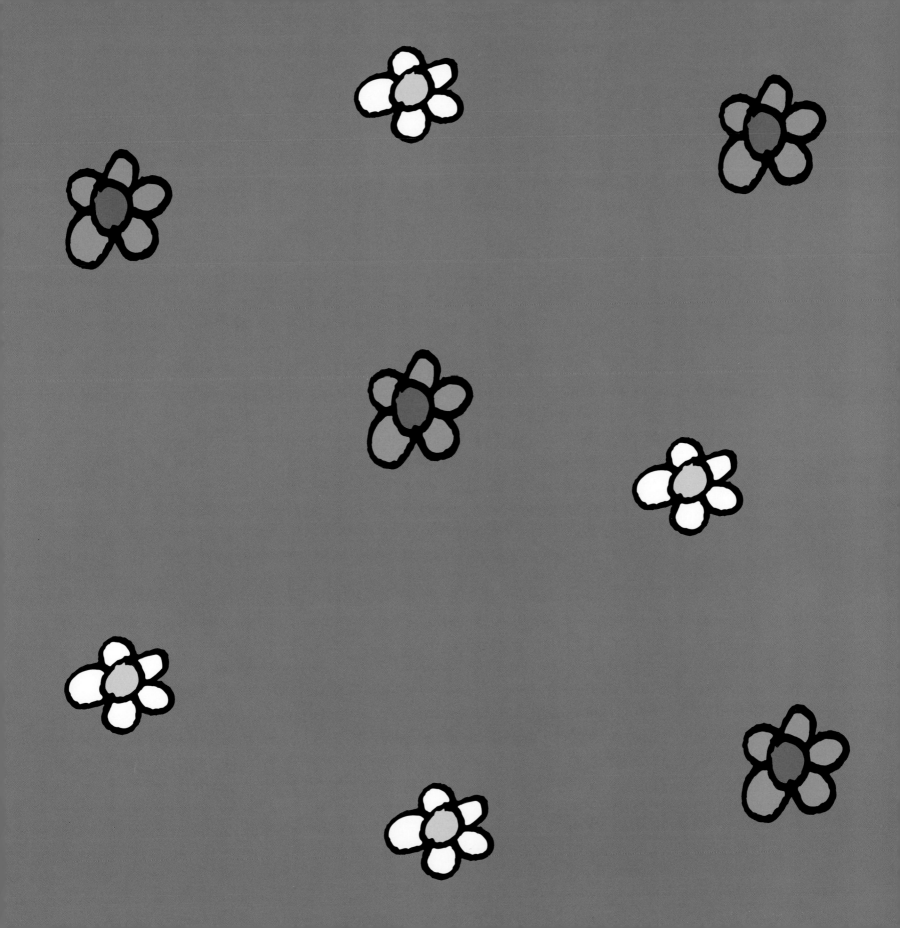

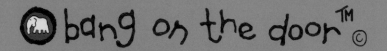

OXFORD
UNIVERSITY PRESS

Great Clarendon Street, Oxford OX2 6DP

Oxford   New York

Auckland Bangkok Buenos Aires Cape Town Chennai Dar es Salaam Delhi Hong Kong
Istanbul Karachi Kolkata Kuala Lumpur Madrid Melbourne Mexico City Mumbai
Nairobi São Paulo Shanghai Taipei Tokyo Toronto

Oxford is a registered trade mark of Oxford University Press
in the UK and in certain other countries

Database right Oxford University Press (maker)

First published 2003

All rights reserved.

British Library Cataloguing in Publication Data available

ISBN 0-19-272564-5 (paperback)

1 3 5 7 9 10 8 6 4 2

Typeset in Freeflow

Printed in China